Bessie loved her daddy,

but he was a radio fanatic.

Bessie loved her mommy,

but she was too busy to play.

Bessie's brother, Olly, was too small
and smelly to be much fun.

And Krishna next door wasn't allowed out much.

But Bessie had Grandma.

Grandma had speckled eyes like birds' eggs, bendy thumbs,
and a crinkle at the top of her nose.

Grandma could do tricks with cards.

She could tame birds.

Grandma and Bessie played hide-and- seek.

They played hopscotch.

But Bessie's favorite game was Count Grandma's Freckles.

Grandma always had time for Bessie.

But one day Grandma got ill and died.

Bessie missed Grandma.

She missed her bendy thumbs and her speckled eyes and the crinkle at the top of her nose.

Sometimes at night Bessie thought she could see Grandma's face in the pattern of the curtain. But in the morning it was gone.

Bessie's mother said Grandma had gone to heaven.

'Where's heaven?' asked Bessie. 'Can she call us?'

Bessie looked at the stars in the night, trying to see heaven, but all she saw were the lights of airplanes.

Daddy said Grandma was now part of nature: the trees and the flowers. Bessie saw Grandma's face in a tree once, but when she looked again it was gone.

Krishna next door said Grandma might be born again as an animal or a bird. Bessie looked hard at all the animals she saw, but they didn't look much like Grandma, although she did see a baby chimpanzee once who looked just like Olly.

Bessie grew up, but she still missed her grandma sometimes.

Bessie fell in love, got married, and had a baby.
The baby was a girl. They called her Rose.

At first Rose looked just like any other baby, but as she grew up into a little girl, Bessie noticed something. Rose had green speckled eyes like birds' eggs. She had bendy thumbs and a crinkle at the top of her nose. When she was three, she got her first freckles.

When she was five, she started to tame birds. She was just like Grandma, only a little girl. And that made Bessie very happy.

Because, suddenly, it was as if Grandma
had never been away.